T0194898

God's Word Through Dexter & Gracie

SALVATION

C.M. NEELS & A.L. MCCOY

WestBow Press books may be ordered through booksellers or by contacting:

WestBow Press
A Division of Thomas Nelson & Zondervan
1663 Liberty Drive
Bloomington, IN 47403
www.westbowpress.com
1 (866) 928-1240

ISBN: 978-1-9736-2937-5 (sc)
ISBN: 978-1-9736-2938-2 (e)

Library of Congress Control Number: 2018906228

Print information available on the last page.

WestBow Press rev. date: 07/05/2018

WestBow
PRESS®
A DIVISION OF THOMAS NELSON
& ZONDERVAN

God's Word Through Dexter & Gracie

SALVATION

C.M. NEELS & A.L. MCCOY

WestBow Press books may be ordered through booksellers or by contacting:

WestBow Press
A Division of Thomas Nelson & Zondervan
1663 Liberty Drive
Bloomington, IN 47403
www.westbowpress.com
1 (866) 928-1240

ISBN: 978-1-9736-2937-5 (sc)
ISBN: 978-1-9736-2938-2 (e)

Library of Congress Control Number: 2018906228

Print information available on the last page.

WestBow Press rev. date: 07/05/2018

WESTBOW
PRESS®
A DIVISION OF THOMAS NELSON
& ZONDERVAN

A Note from the Author, and to the Parents:

Train up a child in the way he should go: and When he is old he will not depart from it (Proverbs 22:6). Please take Some time to look up the verses and read them with your child/ children the bonding benefits are amazing! As parents it is our job to lead them to the Lord. We have such a brief time with them, and they have their whole lives, for their adulthood. We live in such a busy, and stressful times. We must make it a priority as a family to spend time with the LORD!

(Left to Right) Back Row: Pastor Matthew Fox, AL McCoy, Pastor Stan Gustafson
Front Row: CM Neels

God led my daughter Callee, and I to start a series of children books using the King James Version Bible, and the guidance of Pastor Stan Gustafson, and Associate Pastor Matthew Fox from Faith Baptist Church. We would like to take this opportunity to let them know how much we appreciate and love them! Thank-You gentlemen! We pray in the books to come that young people will continue to be inspired in following our Lord, and Savior Jesus Christ where ever

He leads you. God Bless, and good Prosperity in all you do!

GOD'S Word Through Dexter & Gracie

God made everything, and everyone even you! (Genesis 1:1, 2:7, 2:21-23). There was a great wise owl named Dexter. One evening he met a new friend, and her name was Gracie. She was a caterpillar while the two of them were talking Dexter asked Gracie if she knew who God was? She said "No". The wise owl told Gracie how much God loves us. He loves us so much that he gave up his only son (John 3:16) so that all of us could be together in heaven.

When God made everything, it was perfect. He made a "Beautiful" garden, it was called Eden (Genesis 2:8). This is where the first two people lived; Adam and Eve were their names (Genesis 2:22-23)

God said they could eat from every tree in the garden except one (Genesis 2:16-17). They did not listen to God (Genesis 3:1-24). When they ate of the forbidden fruit, they sinned against God. This hurt God very much! They could no longer live in the garden (Genesis 3:23-24).

Because this happened our friendship was damaged. We are all born into sin (Psalm 51:5) because of our betrayal towards God. GOD is perfect, and GOD does not know what it is like to sin. He must turn away from it. Gracie asked, "What is sin"? Dexter told her "Sin is all the terrible things we do".

Dexter and Gracie talked, for hours, and Gracie did not want to hear what Dexter was saying about God. No one had every told Gracie about God, not even her family. She thought to herself "Who is this GOD, and what does he want from me?" She was still so unsure about God.

Sometime had gone by and Gracie had some time to think about all that they had talked about and then Dexter asked Gracie "How was she doing, and did she have any questions about their talk the other day?" With some hesitation, she slowly nodded no. However, she thought silently to herself that some part of her believed there may be something to this "GOD-Thing".

Where did all of this "Beautiful" planet, and universe come from? Can it really be an accident? That takes more faith than believing in one great creator! Dexter agreed. Gracie was still not sure of any of it. She knew she needed to ask more questions to find out the truth. She started with more questions to find out the answers she needed, for the truth. Dexter, what is this about God giving up his only son? Can you tell me about that?

Because of our sin, God sent his son Jesus to pay, for our sin on the cross (John 3:16). Since Jesus death, for us on the cross, we can be forgiven, for our sins (Eph. 1:7). That is the only way to be a loyal friend of God.

Gracie did not quite understand, and Dexter was known to be "The Great Wise Owl" and he knew once he told her about "The Gospel of Christ" God would help her understand, and it would all make sense.

By now Gracie was more curious than ever and God did help her to understand and she was excited to tell Dexter the news that God helped her to understand. Dexter told Gracie that GOD had sent his only son into the world, to save us. Gracie said, "I know why now, but what does this mean for me?" The wise owl told her that there are two births; The first is with our mom and dad, and that is how we come to earth.

The other is a spiritual birth. Gracie was anxious to know, "Why do we need that?" Dexter replied, "It is very important to have a spiritual birth for without that birth we will never see God's kingdom." You see Gracie, it is so people can live forever with God." (Romans 6:23) You know Gracie if you have any fear, or reservations about any of this ask yourself would you like to take a chance on your eternity? Gracie said, "So if we want to be with God forever like he wanted in the beginning, we have to have the second birth." Dexter said, "That is right Gracie".

Dexter went on to tell her; For all of us have sinned (Romans 3:23), and we cannot get into heaven unless we are saved. Gracie said "Saved"? Dexter answered, "Yes remember your second birth, your spiritual birth the other term is saved". "Oh," said Gracie who was paying close attention, still unsure, if she wanted to be saved, but she was full of fear of the unknown and sometimes fear wins. However, she still wanted to know more of the "Gospel of Christ".

Even though Gracie spent hours talking about God, and his free gift of salvation. Gracie started thinking about all that was being spoken of and said to herself "I do not need God, and his gift. God would still let me into heaven without this gift. But Jesus said, "that you must be born again" (second birth) to be a friend of God, and that includes everyone.

God shows his love for us in that Christ died, for us (Romans 5:8). By grace, we are saved through faith (Eph.2:8). Just by believing this we have our second birth. The best part about this beautiful gift God has given us is that we can NEVER lose it (John 6:37), and we do not have to be good to keep it.

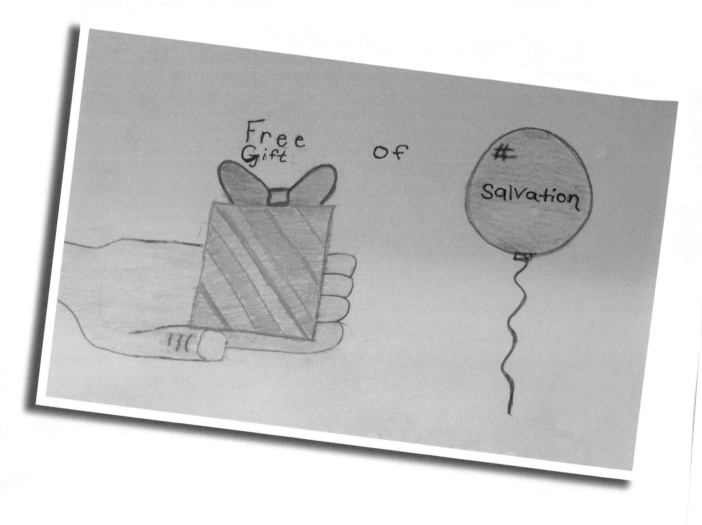

While Gracie was looking inside her heart something "Amazing" was happening to her, she was going through a transformation from a lowly caterpillar into a graceful butterfly (2nd Corinthians 5:17). She had accepted Jesus Christ as her savior, and so it was from that day forward Dexter, and Gracie would gladly tell all whom they met about God, and his wonderful gift. God had brought the two together, and the two had become best friends. Dexter the Great Wise Owl the narrator, and with the help of Gracie, and her beautiful wings that had turned into that pages of the bible.

Thanks, be unto God, for his unspeakable gift. (2nd Corinthians 9:15)

Faith Baptist Church welcomes all and would like to send out an invitation for anyone who would like to attend to worship. We are located at 520 12th St. Moline, IL. 61265

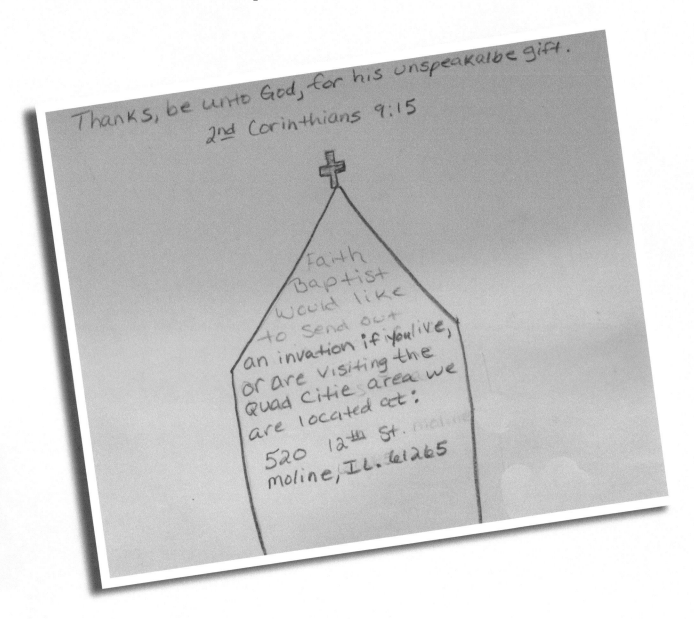

Author Biography

There are two Authors and two Pastors that helped make this book to life. C.M. Neels(daughter) came up with the idea and A.L. McCoy (mother) and together bloomed the characters and the story unfolded from there. Pastor Stan Gustafson and Associate Pastor Matthew Fox edited it to make sure God's word was perfect from the King James Version Bible. Both Pastors are from Faith Baptist Church located at 520 12th St. Moline, IL. 61265.

Printed in the United States
By Bookmasters